Private I in . . .

The
UPPER CASE

TROUBLE IN CAPITAL CITY

Written by Tara Lazar

Illustrated by Ross MacDonald

DISNEP • HYPERION

LOS ANGELES   NEW YORK

To my friends "The Punny Bunch"!
—TL

To the capital folks at Pippin
—RM

Text copyright © 2019 by Tara Lazar
Illustrations copyright © 2019 by Ross MacDonald

First Edition, October 2019
10 9 8 7 6 5 4 3 2 1
FAC-029191-19242
Printed in Malaysia

This book is set in 20-point Columbus MT Pro/Monotype.
Designed by Phil Buchanan

Library of Congress Cataloging-in-Publication Data

Names: Lazar, Tara, author. • MacDonald, Ross
Title: The upper case : trouble in Capital City / by Tara Lazar ;
illustrations by Ross MacDonald.
Description: First edition. • New York, New York : Disney Hyperion, 2019.
Summary: When upper case letters disappear from Capital City, Question
Mark calls on Private I to investigate.
Identifiers: LCCN 2018033074 • ISBN 9781368027656 (hardcover)
Subjects: • CYAC: Alphabet—Fiction. • Punctuation—Fiction. • Mystery and
detective stories.
Classification: LCC PZ7.L4478 Up 2019 • DDC [E]—dc23
LC record available at https://lccn. loc.gov/2018033074

Reinforced binding

Visit www.DisneyBooks.com

I was dozing in my chair when **Question Mark** barged into my office. He looked bent out of shape.

"What's the matter, **Mark**?" I asked.

"Don't ask," **Mark** said. "I'll run out of ink."

True. This town is full of questions.

"I need your help . . . and his help, too!" He grabbed **Exclamation** to emphasize the point.

Finally, **Mark** spelled it out. "All the uppercase letters are missing!"

"That's impossible," I said.

"This is *Capital* City."

"**Private I**, you're the last capital letter standing," said **Mark**.

I sat down. This was serious. If all the capital letters were gone, there'd be incomplete sentences dangling everywhere. The entire city would be thrown into chaos.

Plus, I had to watch my step—I could be next.

I told **Mark** I'd take the case.

It was tough catching up with all the types I needed to interview.

Hyphen was busy dashing around town.

Period was directing traffic.

Ampersand was minding her **p's** and **q's**.

Apostrophe was gathering his possessions.

And **Comma** was dividing her time on a huge list of things.

Luckily, the **Quotation Twins** were willing to talk. "Yeah, something's definitely up, besides us," they said. "But don't quote us on that."

I needed a solid lead. I strolled into Café Uno—
or *afé no* as it was now known.

But my favorite waitress
had been replaced . . .
by her little sister.

She didn't look happy.
"Why so low?" I asked.

"**B** didn't show up for work this morning,"
little b explained.

"**B** is always the second one here.
We don't know where she is."

I was at a loss for words—
especially words starting with **B**.

afé
no

"Here, **B** left this." **Little b** handed me a slip
from **B**'s order pad. It was full of stars.

Aha, a noteworthy clue.

Sometimes **Asterisk** gets mistaken for a star.

So I questioned my old pal **8**, who lives below him.

But we came to a dead end.

After a long day on the case, I sat on my stoop and watched the sky darken. "Oh, **B**, where could you be?"

That's when I noticed a faint glow coming from the old, abandoned part of the city known as Cursive Loop.

First thing in the morning, I took the train out to Cursive Loop.
I circled the winding streets, searching for clues.

A cold wind whipped around me, and I began
to lose hope. Maybe I needed a plan **B**.

But wait, what was this?

I picked up the paper trail and . . .

. . . there they were, high above on the movie marquee.

"Gee whiz, what happened?" I asked.

"Help!" replied **G-Whiz**. "**Exclamation**
stuck us up here and then knocked over the ladder!"

"He promised to put us all in the movies," said **B**.
"I always wanted to see my name in lights."

"Phew! I never thought I'd want to be a lower case!" said **G-Whiz**.

So **Exclamation** was the explanation. "Follow me," I said.
"Could he still be with **Question Mark**?!"

I knew those two together spelled trouble.

The capitals and I barged into **Mark**'s place. Just as I suspected, **Exclamation** was right beside him.

"You're no punctuation mark," I said. "You're just a punk."

"**Exclamation** is crooked!" yelled **G-Whiz**.

"Lock him up and throw away the keyboard!" cried **B**.

"Now, now, let's all calm down," I said. "Everyone stop shouting."

"Exactly!" exclaimed **Exclamation**. "I'm tired of all the shouting. Can't a guy get a little peace and quiet?"

"I don't think he means you,"
I told the little **p's** and **q's**.

"Capital letters are always calling me," **Exclamation** said.

"YES, HA, OMG!" he yelled.

"They want me to join them. As if they aren't loud enough on their own!"

This was mind-boggling.

And earsplitting.

"On the outside, I may look excited, but sometimes I need silence and calm. I want to relax with a good book," **Exclamation** said with a sigh.

I understood his point. I love a good detective story myself.

"I hear you loud and clear," I said. "Sometimes you don't want to be big and brash. But—you're too important to fade away."

"Huh? I'm . . . *important*?"
Exclamation perked up.

"Sure, you're more than just a lot of noise. You're about attention. Respect! In the end, you make a huge impression. You can be a straight, stand-up guy."

Just then, the Grammar Police arrived. "This is totally out of character for you, **Exclamation**," they said. "Come along, we've got to book you."

According to the letter of the law, **Exclamation** would serve a short sentence. Turns out, that cooling-off period was just what he needed.

As for **B**, well, she's always been a star in my eyes.

I had wrapped up another case,
and I hoped trouble in Capital City
wouldn't return.

Famous last words!

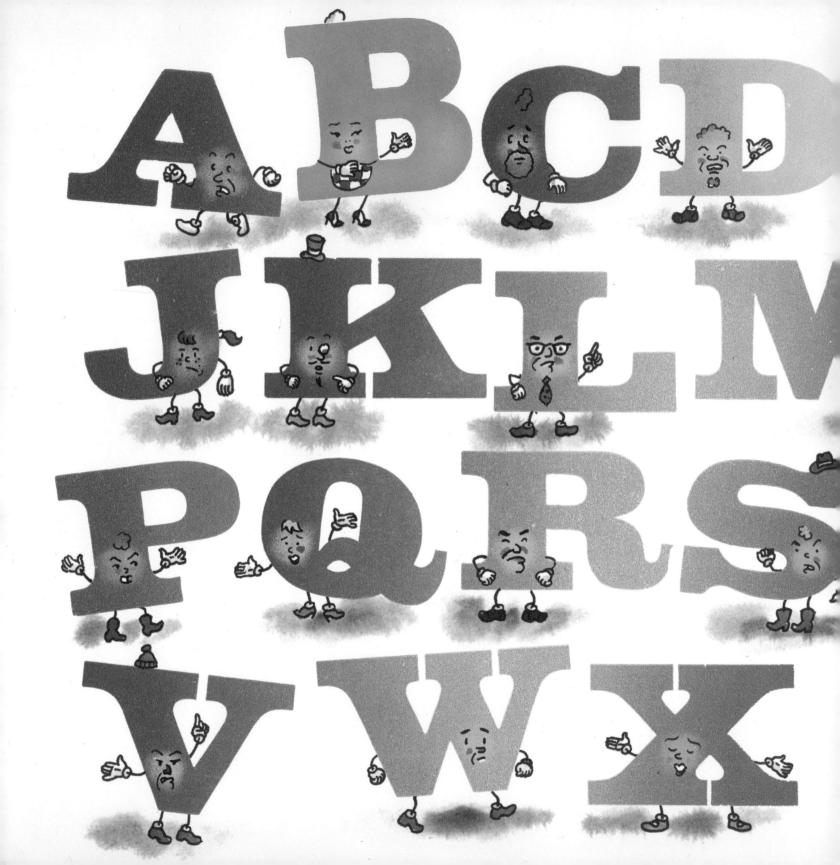